Perfect Pets

written by Rob Domino

illustrated by Tomek Bogacki

Macmillan McGraw-Hill

New York   Farmington

Every day after school Siva waited for her brother, Rajiv. They took the Number 3 bus to Main Street. Then they walked the rest of the way home. They went up the steps to the third floor. They walked down a long hall past the other apartments.

Today Mrs. Russell's dog barked as they walked by. The parrot in room 3B barked, too. It was making the same sound as the dog.

There were lots of pets in the building. Siva and Rajiv's parents had let them have one, too.

"I wish we could get another pet," said Siva.

"You mean, like a dog?" Rajiv asked.

"No, not a dog. A bird!" said Siva.

"What about a flying dog?" said Rajiv. "A dog with wings. We could put him on a string . . ."

". . . just like a kite!" Siva said, laughing.

"We could take him to the park," said
Rajiv. "If a person yells, 'Keep dogs off the
grass!' we'll say, 'But he's not on the grass!' "

"I wish he wouldn't run after little animals," said Siva. "There are hundreds of them in the park."

"Don't worry," said her brother. "They'd be safe. Little animals run up trees when they see a dog."

"But he'd fly after them," said Siva.

"Maybe Rover would just want to play."

"Who's Rover?" asked Siva.

"Our flying dog," said Rajiv.

"Oh, that Rover. But I'd still worry about the little animals. Maybe we should have a different kind of pet."

"What about a goat?" asked Rajiv. "A little goat with horns and nice, long ears!"

"No, I want a white mouse. I'd keep it in my bag."

"You could keep Duke in your bag."

"Who's Duke?" asked Siva.

"A little white mouse with horns and nice, long ears," said Rajiv. "And just think! If a cat tried to run after him, Duke could run at it with his horns!"

"But I like cats!" cried Siva. "I don't want
a pet like Duke. Cats are better. I want a big,
white cat. A really big one. It would weigh as
much as two cats put together."

"Snowball is pretty big."

"Who's Snowball?"

"A cat that weighs as much as two
cats," said Rajiv. "And you know why? She
is two cats, that's why! She has two heads.
One at each end! She never feels alone.
She always has another cat to talk to."

"But what if one Snowball wants to sleep and the other Snowball wants to play?" asked Siva. "What if each Snowball wants to go to a different place?"

"And what if she runs into Duke?" added
Rajiv. "What if she runs into Rover?"

Siva started laughing. "They'll have a party. Rover will eat dog seed. Snowball will use two bowls. But will Duke squeak like a mouse? Or will he bleat like a goat?"

"He'll squeat," said Rajiv.

"What does a squeat sound like?" Siva
wanted to know.

"I'll tell you later," said Rajiv. "Right now,
we'd better think about feeding Sam. You
know how hungry he gets. I'm sure he'll be
happy to see us." He opened up his bag and
searched for his keys.

"It's my turn to feed him," said Siva. Rajiv
opened the door to their home.

They could hear their pet running to
meet them.

"Hello, Sam!" Siva and Rajiv called out.